TRINA

THE MERMAIDS OF ELDORIS, BOOK 2

PJ RYAN

PJRYANBOOKS.COM

ONE

Trina turned over in her shell and watched as tiny bubbles floated through the water beside her. Bubbles fascinated her. They were like their own little worlds inside the water. She often wondered what it would be like to be inside of one.

Did they have secrets too?

Ever since her friend Michelle's crowning, secrets were the only things Trina could think about—the secrets that she had to keep and the secrets that she had yet to discover.

Some time had passed since her adventure into the deep sea with Michelle and Kira. They'd met a few friends and found Michelle's grandfather.

He held the biggest secret of all. There was another world. Not inside of a bubble—not as far as she knew—but above the water.

For all of her ten years, Trina had believed—like most of the other mermaids in Eldoris—that the idea of a world above the water was just a fantasy. She'd never come close enough to the top of the water to imagine that it could be real.

From a very young age, mermaids were taught to always

swim down when possible. Never risk getting too close to the sparkling sunlight that made the water glow.

Now, seeing what was above the water was all Trina could think about.

She sat up in her shell and looked through the water at the other slumbering figures around her.

Since Michelle had moved into the Coral Palace, she and Kira had moved in as well to be her attendants. Trina shared a sleeping space with Kira and many other mermaids that worked there. It was the safest place they could be, but to Trina, it had become a nightmare.

She couldn't sleep. She couldn't focus on anything other than the discoveries she'd made on her adventure with Kira and Michelle.

As she swam quietly through the water, she hoped that she wouldn't wake anyone. She was just about out the door when a tiny voice drew her attention.

"Where are you going, Trina?" A sea slug crawled along the rocky wall of the sleeping space.

"Nowhere, Bea—just for a swim," Trina whispered to her. "Go back to sleep."

"I'm not sleepy." The sea slug raised her head and smiled. "I'll go with you."

"It's better if you don't." Trina frowned. "Just stay here."

"Trina." Bea crawled up along her fingers and onto her arm. "Are you looking for it again? I thought you learned your lesson about that."

"I know it has to be here somewhere. I heard Michelle speaking to her mother about it. I just want to see for myself." Trina stared at the small creature. "You know why I can't let it go."

"I know that you learned too much on our adventure. I know that you haven't been sleeping. But that's no excuse for breaking the rules of the Coral Palace. The queen would not be pleased."

"I don't plan to get caught." Trina smiled and raised an eyebrow. "Unless a noisy sea slug like yourself gets me into trouble."

"I won't say a word." Bea crawled up her arm and onto her shoulder. "But I'm going with you."

Trina sighed. She knew better than to argue with Bea. For such a small creature, Bea was quite stubborn.

She swam through the corridors of the Coral Palace.

Over the past few nights, Trina had been searching for a room that she'd heard Michelle talk about with her mother—a room that held proof of this other world. Trina wanted to see it for herself. She wanted to know once and for all if there really was another world.

She thought about the nearly invisible string that Kira had been tangled in on their adventure. It was like nothing she'd ever seen before. Carlos, a lobster who'd rescued Kira, had called it fishing line. But was he right? Or was that just another made-up story?

After believing that the ocean was the only world that existed for so long, she needed proof to change her mind. That proof, she believed, was in the secret room.

She'd asked Michelle about it, but she had refused to say a word. As a princess of Eldoris, it was Michelle's job to protect all the mermaids and that meant following the rules.

Michelle had become quite the rule follower.

Trina swam down through a corridor. It led to another corridor that she had yet to explore. The deeper she went, the more confusing the many corridors became. It was like a maze and Trina easily got turned around.

Just as she convinced herself that she'd already been in the same corridor three times, she came across a doorway that was covered in thick seaweed.

"This is new." She ran her fingertips along the seaweed. "I've never seen this before."

"Trina, maybe we should go back." Bea crept along Trina's neck to her other shoulder. "If you're caught somewhere you shouldn't be, you might get kicked out of the palace. Michelle wouldn't be happy about that."

"No, she wouldn't." Trina frowned. "But I can't turn back now, Bea. I think this is it. I think I've finally found it!"

"Once you look inside, you'll never be able to look away again," Bea whispered. "You might find something that you wish you hadn't."

"Maybe." Trina wrapped her fingers around a big chunk of the seaweed. "But at least I'll know the truth—finally. I can't keep lying awake at night wondering what's real and what isn't. I have to know if there's another world out there as Michelle's grandfather claimed—as Carlos says there is—and as our queen wants us to believe there isn't." She glanced over at Bea. "You don't have to stay with me. If I get caught, you get caught too."

"I'm not going anywhere." Bea nestled close to Trina's hair. "If you're going to look, you'd better look fast before someone notices that you're missing."

"This is it." Trina narrowed her eyes, then pulled back the thick seaweed.

TWO

Inside the hidden room, the water was murky and dark.

Trina expected something different. Maybe even something magical. She expected shimmering light and something that would stun her. Instead, all she saw were faint shapes and glimmers of smooth surfaces.

"Let me help." Bea closed her eyes. A moment later, a blue glow began to emit from the sea slug. It was bright enough to light up the water around her.

"Bea! I didn't know that you could glow." Trina peered at the sea slug. "You have your secrets too, don't you?"

"I guess I do." Bea glowed brighter. "Hurry and have a look before someone notices the glow."

"Wow." Trina's eyes swept over the variety of items piled up in the space. There were round hard things and long things that looked like stems but would only bend a little to the touch. She ran her hands over a long wooden item that was slim at the top and widened and flattened at the bottom. "What is this?" She noticed the grooves in the wood, as if something sharp had etched a cut into it.

"That is an oar," Carlos piped up from behind her.

"Carlos!" Trina dropped the oar. She spun around as it drifted down to the sand. Her eyes widened at the sight of the lobster who'd crept his way further into the room and the mermaid that swam in behind him. "Kira!"

"Trina." Kira crossed her arms as she looked at her friend. "What have you done?"

"I knew it!" Michelle swam in behind Kira. "Kira told me that you were sneaking around, but I didn't want to believe her. Tonight we followed you. How could you, Trina? You know this place is off limits."

"How could you keep it from me?" Trina placed her hands on her hips. "You may be a princess, but I thought you were still my best friend."

"I am!" Michelle swam closer to her. "I always will be! But you know better than to sneak around the palace. If my mother and father find out that you were here, you'll be in so much trouble."

"If?" Trina clasped her hands together. "Does that mean you're not going to tell them?"

"I should." Michelle frowned. "It's so important to protect all the mermaids from seeing these things."

"Why?" Trina shook her head. "If there really is another world, don't you think that everyone should know about it? It's only right."

"If the other mermaids knew about it, they'd be tempted to make contact with the other world." Michelle looked over the variety of items stored in the small space. "But we know the truth. We know that the human world is a terrible place and that any mermaid that tries to reach it would be in grave danger. It's my job to keep them all safe." She looked back at Trina. "Including you, Trina."

"We don't know that, though. Just because your grandfather said it was terrible—well, that isn't proof that it is." Trina picked up the oar from the sand and placed it back onto the rock it had rested on. "All of these things were created by humans, right?"

"As far as we know." Michelle nodded.

"Well, how can they be so terrible if they can create such interesting and beautiful things?" She reached up and touched a collection of shiny circles that hung from invisible string. "I don't know what it is, but it's just so pretty."

"That doesn't mean they're good." Michelle frowned. "You heard what my grandfather had to say. He said contacting the humans was a big mistake."

"Maybe." Trina turned back to Michelle and Kira. "But how can we know for sure if we don't investigate it ourselves?"

"You know I'm not allowed to leave the Coral Palace anymore. Once I was crowned, it became my duty to protect all the mermaids here." Michelle touched the surface of a smooth, pink object. "Even if we wanted to find out more, I can't leave."

"That's just it, though. How can we expect to protect Eldoris from the humans if we don't know anything about them? In order to keep all the mermaids safe, we have to find out more. We have to know what we're up against. Don't you think?" Trina looked at Michelle. "How can we know how to protect Eldoris, if we don't know who might be attacking it?"

"I suppose you're right." Michelle frowned. "I can speak to my parents about it. But until then, you need to stay out of this room. Understand?" She looked from Trina to Kira. "Both of you."

"You don't have to tell me twice." Kira picked up a long metal pole. "Look at this thing. It must be a weapon of some kind." She shivered as she let go of it. "No, I'm not the least bit interested in looking at any of this."

"I'll stay out, Michelle." Trina grabbed a small tube-shaped item and snapped her fingers. She knew that it would be stowed away for her to access it whenever she needed it. She looked up at Michelle to see if she noticed. If she did, she didn't say a word about it.

"Everyone go back to sleep. I'll speak to my parents about it in the morning." Michelle looked over the contents of the room. "And remember, whether we agree with them or not, the rules are the rules. No one should know about this place. Not a word about it."

"Not a word." Trina nodded.

She followed the others out of the room.

As she swam away, she looked back over her shoulder. She wondered if she would ever be able to find her way back to the room again.

THREE

"Can you hear anything?" Trina craned her neck and swam as close to the entrance of the throne room as she could.

"Nothing." Bea crept higher on the rocky wall. "I know they are talking, but it's too quiet for me to hear."

"This is crazy. We shouldn't be trying to listen in." Kira frowned, but inched closer to the entrance as well. "What if they don't agree with Michelle?"

"I know that I have to find out more. If Michelle can't come with me, then that is just how it will have to be." Trina shivered at the thought. She always tried to put on a brave face, but the truth was, the thought of venturing out into the deep sea again without her friends at her side frightened her. She thought about the giant squid, the octopus, and the enormous shark that she'd encountered the last time. If it hadn't been for the help of her friends, she might not have survived. Would she be able to survive if she was alone?

"Come in, Trina—and you too, Kira." The queen's voice rippled through the water.

Trina froze.

Kira's eyes widened.

"Yes. Yes, I know that you're both out there. Come in, we don't have time to play games."

"Should we?" Trina whispered to Kira.

"We don't have a choice." Kira whispered back. "We've been caught!"

"Let's go, you two!"

An entire wave sloshed toward them, pushed by the force of the queen's voice.

"Right here, my queen." Trina swam into the throne room and immediately bowed down to the queen. She felt Kira swim up beside her and do the same.

"And what do you have to say for yourselves?" The queen stared at them from her shell.

"I just wanted to make sure that Michelle was okay." Trina cleared her throat. "I mean, Princess Michelle." She winced. She was still getting used to that title.

"I see." The queen nodded. "And you as well, Kira?"

"Yes, my queen. Trina and I are both eager to do whatever we can to help Princess Michelle. I'm sorry if that made us a little too nosy." She frowned.

"It's quite alright. I'm glad to know that my daughter has two such loyal friends. We have discussed the matter and the king and I have decided that Princess Michelle's skills are better used in an effort to protect all of Eldoris. Because of that, we have agreed that she can take a journey into the open sea with the two of you. However, we will send a guard with you as well." She gestured to a merman who floated not far from the royal shells. "Bernard will keep the three of you safe. You are to listen to whatever he tells you to do. Understand?"

Trina stared at Bernard. She didn't know him well, but she knew that he wasn't much older than they were. Would he really be any help? She hoped that, at the very least, he wouldn't make things more difficult.

A wave of relief washed over her as she realized that the king and queen had just given them permission to explore. She hadn't thought that would ever happen. Now that it had, her heart pounded harder than ever. What had she gotten herself into? Could she really handle exploring the deep sea in search of more information about the human world?

"I understand, my queen." Trina gave a deep bow to the queen and king. Then she smiled at Michelle as she swam down from her shell.

"We will leave in a few hours, once we've had time to gather the supplies that we need." Michelle swam over to both of them. "That is, if you'd both like to join me. I want you to know that you don't have to. This could be a dangerous journey and if either of you want to stay here, I understand."

"We will go with you." Kira smiled as she took Michelle's hand. "Trina and I would love to be at your side."

"Yes, we would." Trina smiled as well. She did her best to ignore the nervous beat of her heart. She had to be strong. This was her idea, after all.

"Be ready in exactly two hours," Bernard instructed them as he swam past with a snap of his tail.

Trina watched him swim swiftly away. It was hard for her to believe that she would be stuck exploring with him—she already didn't like his bossy nature—but she did think it was best to have some added protection on their journey.

"What's his problem?" Kira scrunched up her nose. "He seems a little tense."

"I think maybe we all need to be a little more tense about this." Michelle swam beside them. "We're thinking of this as an adventure, but the truth is, the closer we get to the human world, the more danger we'll be in."

"At least, that's what we believe." Trina looked at her friends. "We don't know that it's true."

"We only have evidence that it is." Michelle shook her head. "We have to assume that they are dangerous."

"I wonder if they would think the same thing about us." Trina raised an eyebrow. "Do you think we're like a story to them? Just a myth that they can't be sure is true? Something wonderful and scary at the same time?"

"Maybe." Kira tipped her head from side to side. "It's hard to imagine that anyone could find us scary."

"Trust me, it's not that hard." Bea crawled along the back of Trina's neck. "You are the strangest creatures I have ever seen."

"This from a glow-in-the-dark sea slug?" Trina laughed.

"I suppose we all seem a little strange at first." Bea smiled.

FOUR

While the others prepared for the journey, Trina swam off on her own. She even left Bea inside the palace.

Once she was sure that she was alone, she snapped her fingers. The metal tube landed in her hand out of nothingness. She turned it over in her hands.

It was longer than her hand—just about as long as her forearm. It started out narrow and gradually got a little wider at the other end. She noticed that both ends were opened but covered in something that looked like sea glass—but it was far more clear than any sea glass she'd ever seen.

She shook it. It didn't make a sound. She turned it over in her hands again. It felt as if it was hollow. She wondered if she could see right through it from end to end. She put the narrow end up to her eye and pointed the other end away from her.

"Ah!" She dropped the tube and swam backwards at the sight of a giant slug that looked large enough to consume her in one bite.

"Trina? Are you okay?" Bea swam closer to her.

Trina blinked, then stared at the sea slug. She was just as tiny as she'd always been.

"How did you do that?" She narrowed her eyes.

"Do what?" Bea swam down through the water and landed on the metal tube that had settled in the sand. "I knew you took something from that room. You really shouldn't have done that, Trina."

"You were just huge!" Trina crossed her arms. "You never told me that you could make yourself giant."

"What are you talking about?" Bea stared up at her. "I can't make myself any bigger than I am." She looked down at the tube. "What is this thing?" She crawled down to the end of it and peered through the small end. The large end was pointed in Trina's direction.

Trina swam down toward it.

"Ah!" Bea somersaulted through the water and wriggled in pure panic. "Stay back, beast!"

"Bea? It's just me." Trina stared at her.

"No, it's a giant version of you!" Bea opened one eye and looked at her. "Oh good, you're you again."

"I didn't change." Trina frowned. She stared at the metal tube. "It must be this thing. That must be what is making things look bigger." She snatched it up from the sand. "Bea, stay right there."

Trina pointed the large end of the tube at Bea, then looked through it. She shuddered at the sight of the giant slug. Then she lowered the tube. Bea shrank back down into an adorable little sea slug.

"This thing must be magic!" Trina smiled as she looked it over. "It can make things bigger." She pursed her lips. "Actually, it can make them appear bigger. We don't really change sizes, it just looks like we do."

"What would be the point of that?" Bea floated through the water.

"I'm not sure." She put the tube up to her eye again and looked in the direction of the Coral Palace.

Suddenly, Michelle, Kira, and Bernard were right in front of her. Her heart raced as she realized that she'd been caught with an item from the secret room.

She dropped it quickly. When she did, the other mermaids vanished. Confused, she peered through the water. In the distance, she could see faint outlines of her friends and Bernard. Had they been that far away the whole time?

She snapped her fingers so that the tube would disappear. "Maybe it's to help things that are far away seem closer? No time to think about it now, it looks like everyone is ready to go."

Bea climbed onto her shoulder. Trina swam toward the others.

"There is no reason for him to come with us." Bernard crossed his arms as he stared at Carlos. "He'll just slow us down."

"He rides with me." Kira frowned. "Carlos is coming with us."

"I am in charge here and I was instructed to escort the three of you, not a lobster and certainly not that." He pointed at Bea.

"Excuse me?" Bea reared up on Trina's shoulder.

"They're going." Trina looked straight at Bernard. "They both helped us on our last journey. Carlos knows more about the human world than any of us do. Bea can glow in the dark and light our way in dark places."

"She's right, I think it would be best if they came along." Michelle met his eyes. "Are you going to question me?"

"No, princess." Bernard frowned. "Then we should get going. We've already wasted enough time." He swam off ahead of them.

"That's the wrong way!" Carlos called out.

"This is going to be a very long journey." Kira shook her head.

Trina noticed a necklace of gems around Michelle's neck.

"Your mother let you take it?" She smiled.

"Yes, she did—so we won't get lost. Which, with Bernard along, is going to be very important." She laughed as he swam back toward them.

"This way." Carlos pointed his claw through the water. "It will get us closer to where the humans can be seen."

"Stay together." Bernard cleared his throat, then swam in the direction that Carlos pointed.

As Trina swam behind the group, she thought about the metal tube. Someone had created that. It wasn't something that grew, it wasn't made out of natural materials. Someone had invented it, designed it, and then built it. She guessed that the being who created it had to have a brilliant mind. It wasn't a weapon, it was a tool.

Could a human who invented something so wonderful really be all bad?

She guessed that they would find out soon enough. The idea terrified her and thrilled her at the same time.

FIVE

Lost in thought, Trina didn't realize that she'd drifted a bit far behind the others. She wondered if there would be a moment when she would have to confess to Michelle that she'd stolen something from the secret room. Maybe she could return the tube to the room before anyone found out.

"I said stay together!" Bernard swam up to her with a sharp snap of his tail.

The motion sent a ripple of water right into her face.

"Bernard!" She frowned as she ducked. "Relax!"

"It's a simple instruction. Stay with the group. If you can't keep up, then there's still time for you to turn back." He stared at her. "I won't let anyone put the princess in danger."

"I'm not putting her in danger." Trina glared at him, then swam up to her friends. It made her skin prickle to think of being stuck with Bernard for the whole journey. She wondered if there might be a way to leave him behind.

"Are you okay, Trina?" Michelle wrapped an arm around her shoulder.

"I'd be better if Bernard was a bit more friendly." She glanced at him as he swam up to the group.

"We should rest now." He pointed to a pile of rocks nearby. "Stay together. Don't be too loud. Don't make a lot of ripples."

"I'm not tired yet." Kira peered back through the water. "We haven't even gotten that far."

"It's better to rest before you're tired." Bernard sat down on one of the rocks. "Wearing yourself out to the point of exhaustion makes it harder to recover."

"Kira's right, we should go a little farther before we rest." Michelle looked at Carlos. "We still have a long way to go. Don't we, Carlos?"

"Yes, we do." Carlos peeked out from Kira's hair. "We must cross the deep sea before we get close to the shallow sea."

"All the more reason to rest now so that we'll have the strength to get through the entire journey." Bernard leaned back along the rock and looked up through the water. "This whole thing is pointless. We all know that humans aren't real."

"Is that what you think?" Carlos chuckled.

"I don't care what anyone says, no one is going to convince me that there's another world out there somewhere. It's ridiculous. My sister, Avery, talks the same nonsense. She insists that humans are real. But she doesn't have a clue. It's just a fantasy."

"They are real." Trina crossed her arms.

"Oh, really?" Bernard looked at her intently. "Have you seen one?"

"No." Trina frowned. "But that doesn't mean they're not real."

"Yes, actually it does. You can pretend they are, but it's all just imagination." Bernard rolled his eyes. "I just want to get through this and get back home to the real world."

"Why did you even come with us if you don't believe in our mission?" Michelle glared at him. "You should have told my mother how you felt."

"I don't question the queen." He shrugged. "Besides, I don't mind a journey and it's an important job to guard a princess."

"A princess that you think is a fool."

"I didn't say that." He swam up off of the rock. "Let's move on. We've had enough rest."

As they continued through the water, Trina swam up beside Michelle. "Are you sure about this?" She looked over at her friend. "Bernard might make things difficult."

"Just ignore him. The important thing is that my parents trusted us all enough to let us take this journey. We don't want to let them down, do we?"

"No, you're right." Trina smiled at the thought. It *was* nice to be trusted with such a big responsibility. "Do you think we'll actually see a human this time?"

"Enough talking!" Bernard snapped. "You're going to draw the attention of a predator."

"Enough, Bernard!" Michelle put her hands on her hips as she stared at him. "You're here to protect us, not to boss us around."

"You were told to listen to me." He stared back at her. "I'm not bossing you around, I'm making the best decisions I can to keep you safe."

"If you keep making these safe decisions, we're never going to get anywhere!" Trina plopped down on a rock and flipped her tail through the water. "We might as well be going in circles."

"I'm doing the best I can. The three of you don't even know where you're going." Bernard crossed his arms. "How am I supposed to protect you if I have no idea what we might run into?"

"Try to relax." Kira smiled at him. "There really isn't a reason to be so stressed. The open sea is perfectly safe most of the time."

"Until it's not." Bernard narrowed his eyes.

"Uh, excuse me." Carlos waved his claws through the water. "Hello? Down here!"

"Not now, Carlos." Kira waved her hand at him.

"Yes, now!" Carlos clacked his claws. "A little bit of that danger you two are arguing about is headed straight for us!"

"What is that?" Michelle swam back toward Trina.

"Stay back." Bernard turned to face the figure that grew closer and closer. "It's too far away, I can't tell what it is."

Trina's heart pounded. She knew that with the tube she would be able to see what it was. But if the others saw her using it, they would know that she'd taken it. She could be in a lot of trouble.

"I'm going to stop it from getting any closer." Bernard snapped his fingers. Suddenly there was a long thin pole in his hand with a very sharp tip.

"What is that?" Trina gulped.

"It's something the queen gave me to keep you all safe." He looked over at her. "Now be quiet so that I can aim!"

"But it's sharp! It will cut or even kill!" Kira swam closer to him.

"Stay back!" he barked at her.

Trina snapped her fingers as her heart raced. What if the figure that approached was just an innocent sea creature? She couldn't let Bernard hurt it. The metal tube landed in her hand. She put it up to her eye and looked through it in the direction of the figure.

"No!" she cried out. Then she slammed her shoulder into Bernard. "Don't throw that! It's your sister!"

SIX

"What?" Bernard growled as he was knocked through the water.

"It's your sister! Avery!" Trina swam in front of him. "Don't you dare throw that weapon!"

"You're nuts! You can't tell who that is from here! Avery is back in Eldoris!"

"No, she's not." Trina held out the metal tube to him. "Look through this."

"Trina, what is that?" Michelle peered at it.

"Are you sure it's her?" Kira stared through the water. "I can't see at all from here."

"It's a tool. A human tool." Trina lowered her eyes. "It lets you see things that are far away."

"Like this?" Bernard put the large end up to his eye. "I can't see any better!"

"No, like this." Trina turned the tube around for him.

"Avery!" he shouted, then lowered the tube. He stared through the water. "How is that possible? What kind of magic is that?"

"I'm not sure." Trina clasped her hands together.

She felt Michelle's eyes on her.

Kira swam closer. "Where did you get that?" She eyed the tube. "Is it magic?"

"I don't think so. I don't know." Trina looked at Michelle. "I took it from the secret room. I know I shouldn't have, but I was so curious about it. I just wanted to see what it was for. Now that I've figured it out, I think it's pretty amazing."

"You shouldn't have taken that." Michelle crossed her arms. "You know it's forbidden."

"I know. I will tell the queen the truth when we get back. But for now, I think we should use it. It helped me see that it was Avery and not a predator coming toward us, after all."

"Let me see that." Michelle held her hand out to Bernard.

"Gladly. I'm going to go collect my sister." He swam off toward Avery.

Michelle and Kira took turns using the tube. "What do you think it's made out of?" Kira turned it over in her hands. "It's hard like a rock, but light."

"It's metal." Michelle tapped her fingertips on it. "My mother has taught me about a few of the items in the secret room, so that we can keep a lookout for other items like them. I'm not sure how it's made, but it's nothing that can be found in the sea."

"Oh dear, Bernard is pretty upset." Trina watched as he thrashed through the water while speaking to Avery.

"We should go over there." Michelle swam forward.

Trina and Kira followed after her. When they reached Bernard, his shouts made the water ripple around him.

"You are in so much trouble!" he shouted.

"I just wanted to come along." Avery frowned. "What's the big deal?"

"The big deal is that now I have to take you home!" Bernard pointed to the water ahead of them. "Let's go, start swimming!"

"Wait!" Michelle swam in front of him. "If we go back now,

we'll have lost so much time." Michelle looked at Avery. "I think we should let her join us."

"Join us? On this dangerous mission?" Bernard shook his head. "It's out of the question. She needs to go back home. Trina or Kira can take her."

"No." Avery glared at her brother. "I want to continue on with you. I know what this mission really is."

"What it really is?" Michelle raised an eyebrow. "What do you mean?"

"I mean that you're all here to hunt humans. If you find one, you might even hurt it!" She waved her hands through the air. "That's why I followed you—to make sure that you don't."

"That we don't hurt an imaginary creature?" Bernard chuckled.

"They're not imaginary." Avery looked from Michelle to Trina to Kira. "They're not, are they?"

"Whether or not they are imaginary, we would never cause them harm." Michelle swam over to Avery. "Not unless they tried to hurt us first. How do you know anything about them? Young mermaids aren't allowed to know about humans."

"I've overheard my father speaking about them."

"Avery!" Bernard barked. "Don't tell her that, you could get Father in a lot of trouble. Besides, everyone knows he's a little crazy."

"He's not crazy." Avery balled her hands into fists. "He has seen humans. He said so and I believe him."

"Your father has seen humans?" Trina swam over to her. "Are you sure?"

"Yes. He said that he saw a whole boat full of them." She snapped her fingers. A long flat rock appeared in the palm of one of her hands. "Do any of you even know what a boat is?"

"A boat?" Michelle peered at the rock. "That's a rock."

"My father kept this rock. He etched an image into it of

what he saw. He knew that no one would believe him. But this is a boat." She held out the rock to Michelle. "See?"

"What is a boat?" Kira tilted her head as she looked at the rock.

"My father says it's like a giant shell, but it floats on top of the water. Humans ride in it. That's how they can travel on the sea." She looked up at Michelle. "See how it has a curved bottom? That's how it floats."

"This is amazing." Michelle nodded.

"I've never seen anything like it." Trina stared at it. "I wonder if we could make something like that."

"Make a boat?" Bernard threw his hands up into the air. "For what? We're mermaids, we can't live outside of the water."

"I was just curious." Trina frowned. "Michelle is right, we've already wasted too much time. Avery should travel with us."

"Please, Bernard?" Avery looked at him with wide eyes.

"Fine, but only because I want you to see that there are no humans to be found. Hopefully you and Father can put this fantasy behind you once and for all." He snapped his tail sharply through the water as he swam off.

"Avery, you can swim with me." Kira smiled. "As long as you're not afraid of lobsters."

"Lobsters?" Avery swam closer to her.

"Hi!" Carlos popped out from beneath Kira's hair.

"Ah!" Avery swam backwards.

"Don't worry, I'm friendly!" Carlos shouted and clacked his claws.

SEVEN

"Okay." Avery inched closer to Carlos. "If you say so."

"I do." He bowed his head to her. "Welcome to our adventure."

"Thank you." She smiled and bowed in return.

Trina swam ahead of Kira and Avery. She caught up with Michelle.

"I hope you're not too angry with me." She looked over at her.

"I'm not angry." Michelle frowned. "But you should be more careful. My parents have rules, and if you break them, you can get yourself into a lot of trouble."

"I know." She glanced back at Avery. "Do you think her father really saw what he says he saw?"

"He saw something and he etched a picture of it. That means there's something to see." Michelle lowered her voice. "I don't think he would lie about it. But Bernard is right. His father is known to have some strange ideas. It's hard to say."

"What if we don't find anything at all?" Trina stretched her arms out as she swam. "What if we came all this way for nothing?"

"We'll find something." Michelle narrowed her eyes. "I can feel it."

"I hope so." Trina smiled. "Want to race? We can make up for some time."

"I don't think Bernard would like that." Michelle looked over at Bernard, who slashed his arms angrily through the water and flipped his tail more than he needed to.

"All the more reason to do it." Trina grinned. She tapped Michelle lightly on the shoulder. "You're it!" She swam off through the water as fast as she could.

"Hey! That's cheating!" Michelle laughed and chased after her.

"Get back here, you two!" Bernard hollered.

"We're racing too!" Kira sung out. She and Avery began to swim as fast as they could.

"Slow down!" Carlos clung to Kira's hair.

"Unbelievable!" Bernard huffed as he tried to catch up to them.

"Ignore him." Avery rolled her eyes. "He thinks he's so important because he's twelve."

"I heard that, Avery!" he shouted.

"Is he always so bossy?" Kira whispered.

"Most of the time." Avery shook her head. "Mom says it's a phase. But I'm not so sure."

"He's just trying to do his job!" Michelle slowed down. "Maybe we shouldn't make it so hard on him."

"Oh, we're just having a little fun!" Trina grinned. "Maybe he'll loosen up a bit."

"That one?" Bea peered over Trina's shoulder. "I'm not sure that he knows what fun is."

"It's not so easy to figure out when you have responsibilities." Michelle swam a little faster—just fast enough to swat Trina on the back. "Got you!"

"You did!" Trina laughed and flipped through the water. After several turns, Bea squealed.

"So dizzy, so dizzy!" She slid right down Trina's arm and out into the water. "Ah, that's better."

"Sorry, Bea." Trina giggled. She glanced around at the rocks and coral around them. "It looks like we've gotten pretty far in a short time. I don't know about you, but I could use a rest."

"Me too," Kira moaned.

"That looks like a good spot." Michelle pointed to a rock archway. "Look at all the beautiful colors."

"Gorgeous!" Avery cooed. "I never get to see anything like this back home."

"Let's take a closer look." Kira swam toward the colorful plant-like creatures.

"Brr." Michelle shivered. "Is it just me or is the water a little colder all of a sudden?"

"It's not just you." Trina rubbed her arms. "We must have hit a cold spot."

"It feels pretty good after all that swimming." Kira floated through the archway on her back.

"The four of you are impossible!" Bernard huffed as he finally caught up to them. "What was the first rule I told you?"

"Stay together." Michelle smiled.

"Well, we are all together." Trina looked around at her friends, then back at Bernard. "So, I guess you're the one that was breaking that rule."

"You!" He jabbed a finger through the water as he pointed at her. "Just wait until I tell the queen about your human tool and the way you behaved. She will not like any of this!"

"Bernard, try to relax." Avery moaned. "We're just having fun."

"Too much fun can lead to big problems." He stretched out

on a rock. "Now rest, so we can be on our way soon. This cold water means that bad weather might be coming."

"How do you know?" Trina looked at him curiously.

"At home, we're so deep under water that we don't often feel the changes that happen to the sea when weather on the surface changes. But in these more shallow areas, the water can change a lot. The currents will get stronger and the water can get cold or even very warm. Sometimes it will even swirl."

"Swirl?" Kira looked up. "That sounds like fun."

"It's not fun if you're caught in it." Bernard frowned, then pointed up at the water above them. "See that glow? It's from sunlight. The more we can see it, the more shallow we are."

"Wow." Avery stared up at it. "It's beautiful. I want to touch it!"

"You can't touch it." Bernard rolled his eyes.

It was too late. Avery shot up through the water.

"Wait for me!" Trina swam after her. Michelle and Kira soon followed them both. "Ah the water is a little warmer here."

"Catch me if you can!" Michelle laughed as she slapped her tail through the water.

Trina chased after her.

Soon Kira and Avery had joined in as well.

Suddenly Bernard swam toward them. "Stop!" he shouted.

Trina laughed and dove down through the water toward Kira. "I'm going to get you!"

"Stop!" he shouted again. "Please! Listen to me!"

Something in his voice made Trina turn back to look at him. "What's wrong, Bernard?"

Her heart skipped a beat as he pointed above them. "Look!"

She saw a massive shadow. Larger than anything she'd ever seen before. Larger than any sea creature could ever be. It was high above them in the water. The shadow was thick enough to block out the thin tendrils of sunlight that had been drifting down through the water.

"Michelle! Kira! Look up!" Trina's eyes widened as she tried to take in the full length of the shadow. "What could it be?"

"It's a boat!" Avery smiled. "I know it is!"

EIGHT

"A boat?" Bernard shrank back from the shadow. "It can't be."

"Look." Avery displayed her rock again. "It's the right shape." She started to swim upward. "If there's a boat, there must be humans on it. Let's go see!"

"No!" Bernard caught her by the ankle and pulled her back down. "Are you crazy?" He glared at her. "If they see us, we'll never see Eldoris again."

"He's right." Michelle swam up beside Avery. "The humans will want to hurt us. We have to be very careful."

"Maybe it's just a very bloated seal?" Kira swam up to the two of them.

"It's a boat." Trina gazed up at it. "It's a real boat." She swam a little higher than the others. "What do we do?"

"We stay away from it." Bernard crossed his arms.

"Isn't our job to find out more about the humans?" Trina met his eyes. "How can we find out more from down here?"

"Trina, we can't break the surface." Bernard looked at each mermaid in turn. "It is against the law to break the surface. It puts all of Eldoris at risk. All of you know this."

"Maybe you can't, but I can." Carlos floated away from Kira.

"I can't swim all the way to the top, though; someone will have to help me get there. Then you could toss me right up onto the boat."

"No!" Kira shook her head. "That's far too dangerous, Carlos."

"Danger is nothing to me." Carlos clacked his claws. "I may be small, but I am mighty."

"It's too risky." Michelle frowned. "I have no idea what might happen to you if you go up there."

"We all just need to take a minute to think about this." Kira began to swim back and forth. "We found a boat, which is amazing in itself."

"Right now it's just a shadow." Bernard peered up at it. "It could still be something else."

"It could be." Avery stared upward as well. "But it's not. The more time we waste talking about this, the less chance there is that we will get to see a human." She began to swim upward again. "I can only imagine how beautiful they are."

"Michelle's grandfather said they look like us, only with legs." Trina looked down at her long tail. "It must be so strange to have legs."

"Legs aren't the only things different about humans." Michelle caught up with Avery and wrapped an arm around her waist. "They live in an entirely different world. All we know about them is that they are likely monsters."

"You don't know that!" Avery pulled away from her.

"No, I don't know it for sure. But look at the weapon they created." She gestured to the sharp pole that Bernard had snapped into his hands. "What do you think that's for, Avery? Why would they need a tool like that? Its sharp blade is for killing."

"We're using it for protection." Trina swam up to Michelle and Avery. "Maybe that's what they use it for. Avery is right.

This is our one chance to see what humans are really like. We need to take it!" She looked over at Carlos. "If you really want to do this, Carlos, I will take you to the surface."

"Trina, no!" Michelle swam in front of her. "You can't go up there alone!"

"Then we'll go together." Trina stared into their eyes. "We have responsibilities, remember? Our job is to find out what we're up against. That means that we have to be brave and bend the rules sometimes."

"Break the law, you mean," Bernard growled. "If you two are going up there, then I'm coming with you to make sure that you're safe."

"Me too," Avery piped up.

"If Carlos is going, then I'm going with him." Kira swam up to them. "We'll be careful not to break the surface. We have Bernard to protect us."

"You have to promise not to hurt the humans!" Avery turned to face her brother. "Do you promise?"

"I promise that I will only use it to protect us." He locked his eyes to hers. "I will not let them hurt us."

"Calm down." Trina swam upward. "No one is going to get hurt."

As she neared the surface of the water, she noticed a shift in it. It seemed thinner, lighter almost. Her body felt lighter too. It was a strange sensation. The sunlight that poured through the surface of the water dazzled her.

As the others caught up, she watched the giant curved bottom of the boat glide past her. She reached her fingertips up through the water. It was so close, she thought she might be able to touch it.

"Don't!" Bea screeched in her ear. "You don't know where that thing has been!"

Trina jerked her hand back. Her heart skipped a beat. She

was fascinated by the texture and color of the bottom of the boat, not to mention its size.

"We must all be very careful." Michelle swam up beside Trina. "This is new to all of us."

"We can still turn back." Bernard looked up nervously as the boat continued to glide over them.

"We're not going anywhere." Avery smiled as she watched the boat. "I knew they were real!"

"Which means the monsters are real too." Michelle whispered. "The monsters that my grandfather described. They're right above us!"

Trina opened her mouth to disagree, but before she could, a noise louder than anything she'd ever heard shook her entire body. The water vibrated all around her.

NINE

"What was that?" Trina stared up toward the surface of the water. Her stomach twisted with fear.

"I'm not sure." Michelle linked her arm around Kira's.

"I've never heard anything like it," Avery whispered.

"It's the bad weather." Bernard swam closer to the surface. "It's coming." He looked back down at them. "The water is getting darker. When storms come, the sunlight doesn't shine."

"Storms?" Michelle's eyes widened. "That sounds bad."

"It is." Bernard pointed down. "We need to get to deep water as fast as we can. Now!" He began to swim down.

"But the boat!" Avery swam upward instead. "I just want to have one look!"

"No!" Bernard shouted.

"Avery, we need to be safe. If Bernard says we have to go, then we should go." Michelle frowned.

"Bernard has been bossing us around for this entire journey." Trina crossed her arms. "This is our only chance to see this boat. If we swim to deep water, we'll never get back in time to see it again. It's going to pass us by."

"What's the point of seeing it, if we get swept up in a storm?" Kira shook her head. "It seems risky."

"Let's go!" Bernard growled. "There's no time to waste!"

Trina looked up at the bottom of the boat. She was so close that she could count the wooden planks. She wanted more than anything to see what was on it—who was on it. Would she ever have a chance like this again?

"I'm going!" She shot up through the water in the direction of the boat.

"Trina!" Michelle called after her.

"I'm right behind you!" Avery cried out and followed behind Trina.

As Trina got closer to the surface, she heard the loud sound again. Then suddenly the water was lit up by strange white light. She'd never been so scared.

As she stretched her arms above her head to swim upward, she felt a sensation that made her heart stop. Her fingertips pushed through the surface of the water and out into the open air.

Startled by the new sensation, she floated there.

"Trina, are you okay?" Avery swam up beside her but didn't reach up through the water.

"Trina, you broke the surface!" Michelle swam toward her.

"Trina, come back down!" Kira swam closer.

Bernard, with the sharp pole in his hand, swam past them. He floated just beneath the surface of the water.

"Listen to me, things are going to get rough. There will be big waves and lots of loud noises. We have to make sure that we stay together or we might get swept into completely different parts of the ocean." He held out an arm to Avery. "Link your arms together to make sure we don't get separated."

Avery shivered as another loud noise shook the water. She wrapped her arm around her brother's, then Michelle's.

Michelle wrapped her arm around Kira's.

Kira turned to grab hold of Trina's arm, but Trina's fingertips were still above the surface of the water.

"It feels so strange." Trina whispered. She reached her hand a little further out of the water.

"Trina, not too far! What if someone sees you?" Michelle frowned.

"It's time for me to do my part." Carlos let go of Kira's hair and swam toward Trina. "Lift me above the water, I can do the rest."

Trina wanted to know about the humans so badly. She knew that Carlos would learn so much if she gave him the chance. But as another loud sound carried through the water and more white light flashed, a sick feeling in her stomach made her pull her hand back.

"No, Carlos." She looked straight at him. "It's not safe. You're more important than finding out about the humans."

"I am?" Carlos floated in front of her. "Are you sure? Because no one has ever told me I'm important before."

"You're important to me, Carlos." Trina smiled.

"To all of us," Kira added.

"Now can we swim down to safety, please?" Bernard rolled his eyes.

"Yes, let's go." Trina looked over at Avery. "I know how curious you are, but now isn't the time."

"It might be the only chance we get!" Avery moaned.

"I know." Trina nodded. "It's so hard to swim away, but we're not prepared to handle a storm and Bernard is the only one that seems to understand this bad weather. He might have been bossy from the get-go, but that doesn't mean that he's not right."

"Oh no!" Bernard pointed up at the bottom of the boat. "Something's not right!"

The bottom of the boat tilted one way and then the other. Then it tilted very hard in their direction.

"It's going to tip over!" Avery cried out. "It's going to sink down into the sea!"

"Into us!" Michelle gulped. "Everyone swim away from it! As fast as you can!"

Trina couldn't look away from the shifting boat. She couldn't get her body to move. Her tail wouldn't flick. Her arms wouldn't swim. She couldn't think of what to do to get herself to safety. She was aware that all her friends had begun to swim as fast as they could. But she couldn't join them.

"Trina!" Bea squeaked from her shoulder. "You have to swim!"

Bernard glanced back and spotted Trina still near the surface of the water. He swam straight for her.

"Trina! I'll save you!"

TEN

When Bernard's arms wrapped around Trina's waist, she could finally move again.

She swam toward her friends with Bernard at her side. Before she could get far, she heard a loud splash. She looked up in time to see a figure. It descended through the water. It had arms, hair, and a head just like hers. But where its tail should have been were two long legs.

"He's going to see us!" Bernard swam in front of Trina.

"Is that really what I think it is?" Trina couldn't look away from the human as he plummeted through the water.

"It's not a dolphin, if that's what you're asking!" Bernard huffed. "We have to get out of here before he sees us."

"Do you think he's okay?" Trina started to swim toward him.

"Trina! No!" He pulled her away from the still sinking human. "We have to go."

As Trina watched, the human began to swim. He stretched his arms up through the water and kicked his feet quickly. As she watched him get close to the surface, she was surprised by how well he could swim.

Just before he could break the surface, Bernard pulled her down through the water toward the others.

Her mind spun as she realized that she had just seen a human. A real human. Not an imaginary one, but a real one. She didn't know if she would ever see another human again, but she was certain that she would never forget that one.

As she began to swim deeper into the water, she caught sight of something that floated not far from her. She reached out and caught it in her hand. As she stared down at the little figure in her palm, her eyes widened.

"What is this?"

"Trina!" Michelle called out to her. "Get down here with the rest of us."

Trina closed her hand around the figure, then swam down toward her friends. Once she reached them, they all looked back up at the bottom of the ship. It continued to rock, but it no longer tilted. The water no longer vibrated and there were no more white flashes.

"Look." Bernard pointed to the surface of the water. "The sun is back."

Streams of sunlight pushed their way down through the water.

"It's true, it's really true." Avery clasped her hands together. "There is another world out there. Full of humans."

"Humans that would jump at the chance to hurt us if they knew we existed." Michelle frowned.

"That human was brave enough to survive the storm." Kira shrugged. "That's something new we've learned."

"It's not the only new thing we've learned." Trina opened her hand with her palm up. "I think the humans already know that we exist."

"Oh no!" Avery gulped. "Did they shrink a mermaid down into a tiny stone?" She poked at the mermaid figurine, which was attached to a metal loop and a single shiny piece of metal.

"It looks like that." Trina peered at the figure as well. "But I think it's made from something like metal. Only different." She poked at it too. "They did such a good job creating the tail, they must have a good idea of what we look like."

"This isn't good." Michelle began to swim back and forth. "If they know we're here—if they know we exist—that could mean that they're out looking for us. In fact, that boat might have been full of humans hunting for mermaids."

"Do you think he saw us?" Bernard frowned. "If he did, then we just confirmed that mermaids exist."

"I think he was too worried about getting back to the surface of the water to notice us."

"We can only hope that's the case." Michelle wrung her hands. "My mother is not going to be happy about this. Not at all." She looked at the figure again. "What is that attached to it?"

"I have no idea." Trina looked at the shiny object. "It feels like the same stuff that tube is made out of. Maybe it's also metal?"

"Maybe." Michelle looked back up through the water.

Trina looked up as well. She watched as the shadow of the boat coasted out of sight.

"We could have learned a lot more if we'd gone through with Carlos's plan." Trina looked over at the lobster, who was nestled back in Kira's hair.

"It wasn't safe." Bernard swam forward. "My job is to make sure that you all make it back to the Coral Palace safely."

"Now we know boats are real." Avery swam beside her brother. "We know that the human world is right above us. We know that they know about us." She looked back at Trina. "It changes a lot, don't you think?"

"Yes, it does." Trina held the figure tightly in her hand.

"It changes everything." Michelle swam beside Trina. "If the humans know about us—if they know what we look like—then that means we have been seen by more than one human. Which means that some of us have been breaking the law."

"But who?" Kira shook her head. "I can't imagine that any of us would do that."

"Your grandfather for one." Bernard snapped his tail. "He broke the law, that's for sure."

"He didn't break the law. He just followed his instincts." Michelle frowned. "Besides, even if he was seen, it couldn't have been by too many humans. He's very careful."

"We're going to have a big task in front of us when we get back home." Kira narrowed her eyes. "Before we learn anything more about these humans, we need to find out more about the mermaids around us. If some of them are sneaking up to the surface, then we have to find out who and put a stop to it." She shivered. "I've never seen anything so unnerving before. Did you see those legs? The way he swam?" She closed her eyes. "It was scary."

"Scary?" Avery twirled through the water as she smiled. "I thought he was beautiful. Maybe not as graceful as we are, but still beautiful."

"Don't get any ideas, Avery." Bernard looked at his sister. "Kira is right. Humans are frightening. Now that I know they're real, I can only imagine the kind of destruction they probably cause." He snapped his fingers and the long sharp pole appeared in his hands. "Remember, this was created by a human." He pointed to the sharp blade at the end of the pole. "Who do you think that is designed to hurt?"

Trina stared at the blade as it glimmered in the water.

Was Bernard right? If humans were hunting mermaids, then Eldoris was in grave danger. If the human that fell into the water had seen her, then there was a good chance he'd be back. What would happen if they were discovered?

But somewhere deep inside, Trina had to wonder if humans could really be all bad. Somehow she just didn't believe it could be the case.

ALSO BY PJ RYAN

Amazon.com/author/pjryan

*Visit the author page to save big on special bundled sets!

Additional Series:

The Fairies of Sunflower Grove

The Mermaids of Eldoris

Rebekah - Girl Detective

RJ - Boy Detective

Mouse's Secret Club

Rebekah, Mouse & RJ Special Editions

Jack's Big Secret

AVAILABLE IN AUDIO

PJ Ryan books for kids are also available as audiobooks.

Visit the author website for a complete list at: PJRyanBooks.com

You can also listen to free audio samples there.

Made in the USA
Columbia, SC
22 July 2020